STACEY COOLIDGE'S FANCY-SMANCY HANDWRITING

A STORY ABOUT STAYING TRUE TO YOURSELF

WORDS BY
BARBARA ESHAM

PICTURES BY
MIKE AND CARL GORDON

sourcebooks
eXplore

Second grade started out so great.

I liked my teacher, Mrs. Thompson.

I liked my classroom.

And I especially liked Frederick, the class guinea pig.

I'd been waiting since first grade to be a big kid
and have the chance to play with him.

But my feelings changed during the third week
of school—the day we got the red folders.

The folders were filled with lined paper,
and each of us was given a brand new pencil.

That was the day the word
CURSIVE was mentioned.

"Class, today we will begin cursive handwriting exercises," Mrs. Thompson announced.

"Each day we will take time to practice. If you complete your handwriting early, you can read or work on the computer or play with Frederick."

That sounded good to me. I would finally get a chance to play with Frederick. He loved to be held, and he especially loved carrots for a treat.

I was still thinking about Frederick when Mrs. Thompson said, "Everyone open your red folders and take out one sheet of paper. We are going to start by practicing slants and curves. After a few days, we will practice the letters of the alphabet, then we'll move on to sentences, and eventually you will use these folders to keep your own creative writing."

I noticed each of my classmates was looking at their pencil as if it were something new and mysterious, with special powers—like a wizard's wand.

Even Frederick looked nervous.

Then I heard Stacey Coolidge ask, "If we finish extra, extra early, can we play with Frederick AND work on the computer?"

"I don't think you need to worry about that right now, Stacey," Mrs. Thompson answered. "Each student will need plenty of time to practice cursive writing, but if you should finish early, you can play with Frederick and work on the computer."

Stacey was the best at handwriting.
She hardly ever used her eraser.
I hoped Stacey wouldn't get to
Frederick before I did...

I started by practicing my curves and slants, but I wasn't having much luck. I can shoot a basket from where my big brother stands, I can make up my own songs while playing the drums, and I can create complicated obstacle courses to weave through with my skateboard. How could writing a simple curve be so difficult?

And then I heard Stacey say she was finished.
On the first day of practicing, Stacey got to play with Frederick AND work on the computer.

It took us a while to learn all of our letters. A week or two later, we moved on to practicing sentences that Mrs. Thompson gave us to write. Things did not get any easier.

One morning I asked my mom to take me to school early. I wanted to get a head start on my writing practice for the day so I could get a chance to play with Frederick.

I was the first one to arrive.

Frederick was still sleeping.

I pulled a fresh piece of paper from my red folder and started writing my practice sentences. I guess I was holding my pencil too tight, or maybe I was pressing too hard. For whatever reason, my first sentence didn't turn out too well.

Some of the words were too close together. I started to erase, but that made the worst smudge—like a storm cloud filling the sky.

When I tried to erase the storm cloud, I tore a hole in the paper.

One by one my classmates arrived. Everyone started working on the handwriting exercise. I was sure I would be the first one finished since I started before everyone else. Instead, I had a hole, some smudges, and a few worn spots on my paper.

Some of the other kids were having a tough time too. Ben was almost finished when he realized that he was writing on the wrong lines. Mrs. Thompson asked him to start over with a fresh piece of paper.

That's when I saw Stacey Coolidge get up to turn in her paper.

SHE WAS FINISHED!

HOW DID SHE DO IT?

Then Mrs. Thompson said, "Class, Stacey has finished her handwriting and I would like to share her work with the class.

"Do you see how the curves of the b and l are perfectly slanted?

"Notice how the a and e are just touching the center line?"
Mrs. Thompson asked.

"Perfect, **PERFECT**, **PERFECT!**"
I said quietly to myself. "Stacey Coolidge and her fancy-smancy cursive handwriting."

Why is everything so easy for Stacey?

It just doesn't seem fair.

And then Stacey did the unthinkable!

She walked right over to Frederick's cage and fed him a carrot. Then she had the nerve to put him in her lap!

That's why I got here early! So I could feed Frederick a carrot and hold him in MY lap.

I could feel tears filling my eyes, but I held them back.

I was just writing the last word of my cursive sentence when Mrs. Thompson announced, "Time is up. You can finish your work during recess if you like."

My paper looked like it was hundreds of years old—like one of those important documents on display in the history museum. I was embarrassed to hand it to Mrs. Thompson.

"Good try, Carolyn, I am sure cursive handwriting will get easier for you. Maybe you can spend some more time practicing at home."

I did practice at home, but it didn't seem to help. I just couldn't get my hand to cooperate with my brain.

I knew what my handwriting was supposed to look like. I could see it in my mind, but my paper never looked that way when I was done.

Why was cursive so difficult?

After a few weeks of practicing, my cursive handwriting did get better, but not as good as everyone else's.

Mrs. Thompson made a bulletin board for all of her "Handwriting Stars."

Everyone's paper was tacked to the bulletin board on display.

My handwriting was the

WORST

IN THE CLASS.

And it looked especially bad next to Stacey's perfect fancy-smancy writing.

Did Mrs. Thompson see how hard I was working?

Did she see how many erasers I'd worn out?

Did she see the big bump on the finger next to my thumb?

Would I ever be able to write in cursive?

Would I ever get to go to the third grade?

Would I ever get to play with Frederick?

One day, Mrs. Thompson asked if she could speak to me after school. I was sure that she wanted to talk to me about my handwriting. I just knew it.

"Carolyn, you seem to be a bit sad lately. Is there something that you would like to talk about?" Mrs. Thompson asked.

"No, Mrs. Thompson, I just don't know what to do about my handwriting. It's the worst in the class. I look at Stacey Coolidge's perfect cursive handwriting, then I look at mine. Mine is terrible," I said with my shaky, "about to cry" voice.

"Carolyn, you are quite a smart little girl. I can see how hard you have been trying and I am so proud of you.

"Cursive handwriting is something we need to practice. It is a tool for our learning toolbox. And even though it's an important tool to have, no one is ever expected to be perfect at it," she said with one of her "serious" smiles.

"That doesn't mean you should stop practicing or trying to improve. Each of us is better at some things than at others. Stacey has great handwriting, but she probably can't ride a skateboard as well as you. Remember, practice is not meant to make us perfect.

"Besides, some of the most talented poets and writers are not known for their perfect penmanship. They're known for their creativity and storytelling."

"So I don't have to have perfect cursive handwriting?"
I asked, starting to feel better.

"Oh, Carolyn, of course not. Nobody has perfect handwriting.
I do want you to keep practicing and improving. But promise
me that you will not focus on comparing your writing with
others and that instead you'll focus on doing the best that
you can do," Mrs. Thompson said with her most serious look.

"Oh, I promise, Mrs. Thompson!"

"Our next assignments will be writing your own creative stories," Mrs. Thompson said. "Do you have any ideas for what you'd like to write about?"

"I have lots of ideas!" I said. "I can't wait to write them down!" Now I was feeling excited about my next writing project.

"Great!" said Mrs. Thompson. "Speaking of ideas—I think I have one of my own. Just for fun, we can try writing on something other than paper. It will be a new challenge for everyone! Let's celebrate creative writing in all its forms!"

"Now, there's another reason that I wanted to speak with you," said Mrs. Thompson. "I was wondering if you would consider taking Frederick home with you for the weekend. School will be closed on Monday and I wouldn't want to leave Frederick alone for that long."

"REALLY?

FOR REAL?

I can take Frederick home with me for the whole weekend and Monday too?"

I couldn't believe it!

I'm really glad that Mrs. Thompson and I had a talk about cursive handwriting. I will always try my best, but I'm not going to feel bad about what my handwriting looks like.

Who knows, maybe I'll even be a writer one day.

Of course, I'll need to write in my spare time because
I'll be very busy taking care of my very own...

GUINEA PIG FARM!

ARE YOU AN EVERYDAY GENIUS TOO?

Everyday geniuses are **creative**, STRONG, thoughtful, and sometimes learn a little differently from others. And that's what makes them so special!

In *Stacey Coolidge's Fancy-Smancy Handwriting,* Carolyn is having a lot of trouble with her cursive. Other kids in the class are much faster and better at it than she is, even though she practices a lot at home and even goes to school early to practice.

Have you ever struggled with learning something new? What happened?

Carolyn is good at other things like riding her skateboard or shooting baskets. What are some things that you're really good at?

There is a phrase people say when learning something new: "practice makes perfect." But perfection is not always something we should hope for or expect to achieve. And it's really not possible. Nobody's perfect.

Carolyn is frustrated and sad about not being as good as Stacey Coolidge. She worries that her handwriting is the worst in the whole class. But rather than worry about how "perfect" her writing skills are, Carolyn's teacher says that she should focus on becoming a creative writer. Being creative does not mean you need "perfect" handwriting. Handwriting is just a tool in the learning toolbox. The most important part of writing is to share your ideas, thoughts, and feelings.

Of course, Carolyn will still practice her writing. But it's important to remember that we shouldn't compare ourselves to other people's versions of success. It's ok to celebrate the things we do well. And we don't have to strive for perfection. As long as we're trying and making progress, we will accomplish amazing things.

If you or someone you know is struggling to learn something or is worried about their progress, or you feel hopeless about something you're trying to do, please talk about it with a caring adult.

Remember, everyday geniuses are creative, strong, thoughtful, and sometimes learn a little differently from others. It's never a bad thing to be different—embracing and learning from our differences is what makes the world a better place!

ABOUT THE AUTHOR

Author Barbara Esham was one of those kids who couldn't resist performing a pressure test on a pudding cup. She has always been a "free association" thinker, finding life far more interesting while in a state of abstract thought. Barbara lives on the East Coast with her three daughters. Together, in Piagetian fashion, they have explored the ideas and theories behind the definitions of intelligence, creativity, learning, and success. Barb researches and writes from her home office in the spare time available between car pools, homework, and bedtime.

ABOUT THE ILLUSTRATORS

Cartooning has brought Mike Gordon acclaim in worldwide competitions, adding to his international reputation as a top humorous illustrator. Since 1993 he has continued his successful career based in California, gaining a nomination in the prestigious National Cartoonist Society Awards. Mike is the renowned illustrator for the wildly popular book series beginning with *Do Princesses Wear Hiking Boots?* Mike collaborates with his son Carl Gordon from across the world. They have been a team since 1999. Mike creates the line illustrations, and the color is applied by Carl using a graphics tablet and computer. Carl has a degree in graphic art and currently lives in Cape Town, South Africa, with his wife and kids.

Text © 2008, 2018, 2024 by Barbara Esham
Illustrations © 2008, 2018, 2024 by Mike Gordon
Illustrations by Mike and Carl Gordon
Cover design by Travis Hasenour
Cover and internal design © 2018, 2024 by Sourcebooks
Sourcebooks and the colophon are registered trademarks of Sourcebooks.

Published by Sourcebooks eXplore, an imprint of Sourcebooks Kids
P.O. Box 4410, Naperville, Illinois 60567-4410
(630) 961-3900
sourcebookskids.com
Originally published as *Stacey Coolidge's Fancy-Smancy Cursive Handwriting* in 2008 in the United States of America by Mainstream Connections Publishing. This edition issued based on the hardcover edition published in 2018 in the United States of America by Sourcebooks Kids.
Cataloging-in-Publication Data is on file with the Library of Congress.

Source of Production: Lightning Source, Inc., La Vergne, TN, USA
Date of Production: May 2024
Run Number: 5040830

Printed and bound in the United States of America.
LSI 10 9 8 7 6 5 4 3 2 1

Printed in the USA
CPSIA information can be obtained
at www.ICGtesting.com
CBHW080351220424
7193CB00001B/8